WITHDRAWN

House,
Bridge,
Fountain,
Gate

Also by Maxine Kumin

POETRY

Halfway
The Privilege
The Nightmare Factory
Up Country: Poems of New England

FICTION

Through Dooms of Love
The Passions of Uxport
The Abduction
The Designated Heir

House, Bridge, Fountain, Gate

MAXINE KUMIN

The Viking Press   New York

First published in 1975 in a hardbound and paperbound
edition by The Viking Press, Inc., 625 Madison Avenue, New
York, N.Y. 10022

Published simultaneously in Canada by
The Macmillan Company of Canada Limited

Library of Congress Cataloging in Publication Data

Kumin, Maxine W
 House, bridge, fountain, gate.

 (A Viking compass book; C592)
 Poems.
 I. Title.
PS3521.U638H6   811'.5'4   75-1353
ISBN 0-670-37996-4
ISBN 0-670-00592-4 pbk.

Printed in U.S.A.

Acknowledgment is made to Insel Verlag for the quotation
from *Duineser Elegien* from *Sämtliche Werke*, Volume I, by
Rainer Maria Rilke. Copyright © 1955 by Insel Verlag,
Frankfurt Am Main.

 Some of these poems have previously appeared in the
following periodicals: *American Poetry Review, Antaeus,
Arts in Society, The Atlantic Monthly, Boston Arts Review,
Boston University Journal, Crazy Horse, Lynx, Harper's,
Massachusetts Review, Ms., Mundus Artium, New American
Review, New Hampshire Library Bulletin, The New
Republic, Paintbrush, Poetry, The Poetry Miscellany.*

 "Running Away Together" originally appeared in *The
New Yorker.* "Thinking of Death and Dogfood" originally
appeared in *The New Yorker* under the title "Address to an
Old Horse."

In memoriam
Anne Sexton
1928–1974

Sind wir vielleicht hier, um zu sagen:
Haus, Brücke, Brunnen, Tor. . . .
   —Rainer Maria Rilke, *Ninth Duino Elegy*

It is as though things are trying to express themselves through us. It may be, as a poet had said, we are here only to say, house, bridge, fountain, gate.
   —Louis Simpson, *North From Jamaica*

CONTENTS

■

■■ THE KENTUCKY POEMS

III

IV

tacking veils onto felt forms.
Mamselle is an artist.
She can copy the Eiffel Tower
in feathers with a rolled-up brim.
She can make pyramids out of cherries.
Mamselle wears cheese boxes on her feet.
Madame can buy and sell her.
If daughters were traded among the accessories
in the perfumed hush of Bonwit Teller's
she'd have replaced me with a pocketbook,
snapped me shut and looped me over
her Hudson seal cuff: me of the chrome-wire mouth,
the inkpot braids, one eye that looks
wrongly across at the other.
O Lady of the Chaise Longue,
O Queen of the Kimono,
I disappoint my mother.

Adam and Eve and Pinch Me Flat
went to the push-nickel automat.
Adam and Eve had nickels to spend
but who do you think got left at the end?

Two more years of Kaltenborn's reports
and Poland will fall, the hearts
of horses will burst in a battle with tanks.
Soon enough the uncles will give thanks
for GI uniforms to choose
and go off tough as terriers to dig their holes.
Warsaw will excrete its last Jews.

My father will cry like a child.
He will knuckle his eyes, to my terror,
over the letters that come from the grave
begging to be sponsored, plucked up, saved.
I hoard tinfoil, meanwhile.
I knit for Britain's warriors.
This is the year that my mother stiffens.
She undresses in the closet giving me
her back as if I can't see
her breasts fall down like pufferfish,
the life gone out of their crusty eyes.
But who has punctured the bathroom light?
Why does the mattress moan at night
and why is nothing good
said of all the business to come
—the elastic belt with its metal tongue—
when my body, that surprise,
claps me into my first blood?

Adam and Eve and Pinch Me Dead
coasted down Strawberry Hill on a sled.
Adam and Eve fell off in the mud
but who do you think got covered with blood?

SPERM

You have to admire the workmanship of cousins.
There is a look in our eyes.
Once we were all seventeen of us naked as almonds.
We were all suckled except for Richard
who had to be raised on a glue of bananas.
Now he is bald and breathes through the nose
like an air conditioner but he too
said goodnight, Grandfather, when
we were all sheep in the nursery.
All of those kisses like polka dots
touched to the old man's wrinkles
while his face jittered under our little wet mouths
and he floated to the top of his palsy
sorting out Jacob from Esau.

O Grandfather, look what your seed has done!
Look what has come of those winter night gallops.
You tucking the little wife up
under the comforter that always leaked feathers.
You coming perhaps just as the trolley
derailed taking the corner at 15th Street
in a shower of blue sparks, and Grandmother's
corset spread out like a filleted fish

to air meanwhile on the window sill.
Each time a secret flourished under those laces
she eased the bones from their moorings
and swelled like the Sunday choir.
Seven sons, all with a certain
shy hood to the eye. I call it the Hummel effect.

But here, in the next generation,
I'm waiting in line at the Sedgwick
with Hester and Laura to see
Our Gang and a Shirley Temple special.
The Sedgwick has stars on the ceiling
and Shirley has banana curls.
If you have to go to the Ladies
Hester says to sit in the air
or else you will catch something awful
Hester says, even a baby.
It is Saturday. I come out in the sun
with a guilty headache while down the street
at the Lutheran Home for Incurable Orphans
a girl my age wet the bed
and stands draped in the sheets to be punished
and she could have been me.
In three years Laura will wake with
a headache that walks down her neck stem
and puts her into a wheelchair.
She grows patient as an animal.
After that I prefer not to know her.

After that, as important as summer,
the southern branch comes north to visit.

There's Sissy and Clara and Rosie
jiggling on pogo sticks, jiggling
in identical pink under-vests
while Nigger, their loyal Labrador
goes after hoptoads in the garden.
I see a brown stain on Sissy's petticoat.
I see that smart alec, Teddy
playing games behind the furnace
with Clara. They touch in the coal bin.
He gets ten smacks with the hairbrush
and his plane goes down in the Aleutians.
Arthur's still sucking his thumb,
the same arm he loses in Italy.
Meanwhile Frederick and Ben
are born and done up in nappies.
When Frederick is sponged in the basin
and laughs, according to Rosie,
even his little beard wiggles.
Ben buttons up in the Navy
and comes home with five darling ribbons.

Such darlings, those wicked good boys
all but one come to their manhood:
Bo palming poker chips in the frat house,
Joseph gone broody with bourbon,
Michael following the horses
while nursing an early heart murmur,
Alan surprised at the Bide-A-Wee
with an upstate minister's daughter
and diffident James in the closet

trying on Sukey's garter belt,
pulling on Sukey's stockings.

O Grandfather, what is it saying,
these seventeen cousins german
descending the same number of steps
their chromosomes tight as a chain gang
their genes like innocent porters
a milk churn of spermatozoa?
You have to admire the product—
bringing forth sons to be patriots
daughters to dance like tame puppets—
half of them dead or not speaking
while Sukey and James, the end of the line
keep house in the gentlest tradition
of spinster and bachelor sweetheart.
Memory dances me backward,
back to your dining room table
added onto to cross the front hall.
It's a squeeze play of damask on damask.
We're all wearing your hooded eyes
as you ask your aphasic blessing
over thirty-two spoons for the pudding.

THE DEATHS OF THE UNCLES

I am going backward in a home movie.
The reel stutters and balks before it takes hold
but surely these are my uncles spiking the lemonade
and fanning their girls on my grandmother's veranda.
My uncles, innocent of their deaths, swatting
the shuttlecock's white tit in the Sunday twilight.
Some are wearing gray suede spats, the buttons
glint like money. Two are in checkered knickers,
the bachelor uncle in his World War One puttees
is making a mule jump for the cavalry, he is crying
Tuck, damn you, Rastus, you son of a sea cook!
How full of family feeling they are, their seven
bald heads coming back as shiny as an infection,
coming back to testify like Charlie Chaplin,
falling down a lot like Laurel and Hardy.
Stanley a skeleton rattling his closet knob
long before he toppled three flights with Parkinson's.
Everyone knew Miss Pris whom he kept in rooms
over the movie theater, rooms full of rose water
while his wife lay alone at home like a tarnished spoon.
Mitchell the specialist, big bellied, heavy of nose,
broad as a rowboat, sniffed out the spices.
Shrank to a toothpick after his heart attack,

fasted on cottage cheese, threw out his black cigars
and taken at naptime died in his dressing gown
tidy in paisley wool, old pauper thumb in his mouth.
Jasper, the freckled, the Pepsodent smiler,
cuckold and debtor, ten years a deacon
stalled his Pierce Arrow smack on a railroad track
while the twins in their pram cried for a new father.
The twins in their pram as speechless as puppies.
O run the film forward past Lawrence the baby,
the masterpiece, handsomest, favorite issue.
Cover the screen while the hats at his funeral
bob past like sailboats, like black iron cooking pots.
Larry the Lightheart dead of a bullet
and pass over Horace, who never embezzled,
moderate Horace with sand in his eyelids
so we can have Roger again, the mule trainer
crying *son of a sea cook!* into his dotage,
wearing the Stars and Stripes next to his hearing aid,
shining his Mason's ring, fingering his Shriner's pin,
Roger the celibate, warrior, joiner

but it was Dan Dan Dan the apple of my girlhood
with his backyard telescope swallowing the stars,
with the reedy keening of his B-flat licorice stick,
Dan who took me teadancing at the Adelphia Club,
Dan who took me boating on the Schuylkill scum,
Dan who sent the roses, the old singing telegrams
and cracked apart at Normandy leaving behind
a slow-motion clip of him leading the conga line,
his white bucks in the closet and a sweet worm in my heart.

THIS DAY WILL SELF-DESTRUCT

A man lies down in my mind.
We have just made love.
It went historically well, the kind
of hand-in-glove
expertise team workouts can evoke.
Now we lie still and smoke,
the ashtray on my belly blue
as chicory in the dixie cup
on the deal bureau. True,
it's a borrowed room. Third-floor walk-up
as a matter of fact,
foreign enough to enhance the act.
Say it's Grand Forks, where I've never been.
All this takes place in the head,
you understand. I play to win
back wicked afternoons in bed,
old afternoons that were
shadows on the grass longer
than home runs lofted out of the park.
We smoke. The chicory blue goes dark,
the ashtray deepens
and the sun drops
under the rim the way it happens

like a used-up lollipop
and the room goes blind
and a man
a man lies down in my mind.

LIFE'S WORK

Mother my good girl
I remember this old story:
you fresh out of the Conservatory
at eighteen a Bach specialist
in a starched shirtwaist
begging permission to go on tour
with the nimble violinist you were
never to accompany and he
flinging his music down
the rosin from his bow
flaking line by line
like grace notes on the treble clef
and my grandfather
that estimable man I never met
scrubbing your mouth with a handkerchief
saying no daughter of mine
tearing loose the gold locket
you wore with no one's picture in it
and the whole German house on 15th Street
at righteous whiteheat . . . .

At eighteen I chose to be a swimmer.
My long hair dripped through dinner
onto the china plate.

My fingers wrinkled like Sunsweet
yellow raisins from the afternoon workout.
My mouth chewed but I was doing laps.
I entered the water like a knife.
I was all muscle and seven doors.
A frog on the turning board.
King of the Eels and the Eel's wife.
I swallowed and prayed
to be allowed to join the Aquacade
and my perfect daddy
who carried you off to elope
after the fingerboard snapped
and the violinist lost his case
my daddy wearing gravy on his face
swore on the carrots and the boiled beef
that I would come to nothing
that I would come to grief . . . .

Well, the firm old fathers are dead
and I didn't come to grief.
I came to words instead
to tell the little tale that's left:
the midnights of my childhood still go on
the stairs speak again under your foot
the heavy parlor door folds shut
and "Au Clair de la Lune"
puckers from the obedient keys
plain as a schoolroom clock ticking
and what I hear more clearly than Debussy's
lovesong is the dry aftersound
of your long nails clicking.

THE ABSENT ONES

The two foals sleep back to back
in the sun like one butterfly.
Their mothers, the mares, have weaned them,
have bitten them loose like button thread.

The beavers have forced their kit
out of the stick house; he waddles
like a hairy beetle across the bottom land
in search of other arrangements.

My mother has begun to grow down,
tucking her head like a turtle.
She is pasting everyone's name
on the undersides of her silver tea service.

Our daughters and sons have burst
from the marionette show
leaving a tangle of strings
and gone into the unlit audience.

Alone I water the puffball patch.
I exhort the mushrooms to put up.
Alone I visit the hayfield.

I fork up last summer's horse-apples
to let the seeds back in the furrow.

Someone comes toward me—a shadow.
Two parts of a butterfly flicker
in false sun and knit together.
A thigh brushes my thigh.
The stones are talking in code.

I will braid up the absent ones like onions.
The missing I will wrap like green tomatoes.
I will split seventy logs for winter,
seven times seven times seven.

This is the life I came with.

THE KENTUCKY POEMS

THE JESUS INFECTION

Jesus is with me
on the Blue Grass Parkway going eastbound.
He is with me
on the old Harrodsburg Road coming home.
I am listening
to country gospel music
in the borrowed Subaru.
The gas pedal
and the words
leap to the music.
O throw out the lifeline!
Someone is drifting away.

Flags fly up in my mind
without my knowing
where they've been lying furled
and I am happy
living in the sunlight
where Jesus is near.
A man is driving his polled Herefords
across the gleanings of a cornfield
while I am bound for the kingdom of the free.
At the little trestle bridge that has no railing
I see that I won't have to cross Jordan alone.

Signposts every mile exhort me
to Get Right With God
and I move over.
There's a neon message blazing
at the crossroad
catty-corner to the Burger Queen:
Ye Come With Me.
Is it well with my soul, Jesus?
It sounds so easy
to be happy after the sunrise,
to be washed in the crimson flood.

Now I am tailgating
and I read a bumper sticker
on a Ford truck full of Poland Chinas.
It says: Honk If You Know Jesus
and I do it.
My sound blats out for miles
behind the pigsqueal
and it's catching in the front end,
in the axle,
in the universal joint,
this rich contagion.

We are going down the valley on a hairpin turn,
the swine and me, we're breakneck in
we're leaning on
the everlasting arms.

LIVING ALONE WITH JESUS

Can it be
I am the only Jew residing in Danville, Kentucky,
looking for matzoh in the Safeway and the A & P?
The Sears Roebuck salesman wrapping my potato masher
advises me to accept Christ as my personal saviour
or else when I die I'll drop straight down to hell,
but the ladies who come knocking with their pamphlets
say as long as I believe in God that makes us
sisters in Christ. I thank them kindly.

In the county there are thirty-seven churches
and no butcher shop. This could be taken
as a matter of all form and no content.
On the other hand, form can be seen as
an extension of content, I have read that,
up here in the sealed-off wing where my three rooms
are threaded by outdoor steps to the downstairs world.
In the open risers walnut trees are growing.
Sparrows dipped in raspberry juice
come to my one window sill. Cardinals
are blood spots before my eyes.
My bed is a narrow canoe with a fringy throw.
Whenever I type it takes to the open sea

and comes back wrong end to.
Every morning the pillows produce tapioca.
I gather it up for a future banquet.

I am leading a meatless life. I keep
my garbage in the refrigerator. Eggshells
potato peels and the rinds of cheeses nest
in the empty sockets of my daily grapefruit.
Every afternoon at five I am comforted
by the carillons of the Baptist church next door.
I let the rock of ages cleave for me on Monday.
Tuesday I am washed in the blood of the lamb.
Bringing in the sheaves on Wednesday keeps me busy.
Thursday's the day on Christ the solid rock I stand.
The Lord lifts me up to higher ground on Friday so that
Saturday I put my hands in the nail-scarred hands.
Nevertheless, I stay put on the Sabbath. I let
the whiskey bottle say something scurrilous.

Jesus, if you are in all thirty-seven churches,
are you not also here with me
making it alone in my back rooms like a flagpole sitter
slipping my peanut shells and prune pits into the Kelvinator?
Are you not here at nightfall
ticking in the box of the electric blanket?
Lamb, lamb, let me give you honey on your grapefruit
and toast for the birds to eat
out of your damaged hands.

THE KNOT

Lately I am changing houses like sneakers and socks.
Time zones wrinkle off me casually.
I have put aside with the laundry
a row of borrowed kitchens, look-alikes
in which I crack the eggs and burn the toast
but even in Danville, Kentucky, my ghosts
come along, they relocate as easily as livestock
settling in another field. They are a dumb show
of Black Angus, and the unexpected snow
makes angels sit on their stone backs.

Angel of my cafard, displaced daughter, it was
an out-of-season snow we walked in
arms locked, two weeks ago, in the Ardennes
dreamy as soothsayers, along the Meuse
where the World War One monuments, Adonises
and sloe-eyed angels softened with verdigris,
have been updated with the names of all
those who died in labor camps
or up against the wall.
At Bastogne the wind mourned from the swamp.
A giant alarm clock ticked in the Hall
of the States, half Parthenon,
half Stonehenge, hugely American

and here I was the least at home of all
the alien places, alien beds
in the presence of my generation's dead.

This antebellum manse was built in 1836.
Sam McKee, the owner, cut his name
with a diamond on the parlor windowpane.
The glass has run with age and plays me tricks.
A stray cat overlaps my pillow again
and our cat comes back, the one named Rosencrantz,
who chose your open drawer of lollipop pants,
that cotton jumble of fruit-flavor drops,
for her first litter. She brought each forth
in a purple bubble, and ate up all the afterbirth
leaving only a damp stain in the shape
of a splayed-out frog on the top pair. Lime.

Lollipop girl, I hold back out of time
the death of your first dog gassed at the vet's
for biting one-two-three strangers single file
the one day of his life he had regrets
or maybe the one day of his true dog guile.
A stroke, they said, an insult to the brain
and I hear the lie erupt you caught me in:
he's gone to live on a farm, I said, a farm
the vet found. The dream-lie of our lives
what with the way animals come
up in everything I touch of you
and death astride them anyhow.
I told the lie that saved.

And there were turtles from the five and dime
carrying the fatal parasite
that ate holes in their shells, time
after time, shells growing light as lace
as one by one their hearts winked out
like the last orange eyes in the fireplace.
And this year, the new dog, the only other
dog of our days, our rootstock and our fable
now getting up backwards, the smother
of old age seizing him under the table
stuffing his ears and glazing his eyes
like great cracked aggies holding in surprise.

My arms are heavy. They hang down simian style.
I have been swimming again. I swim
to put down the cafard. The college pool
at 82 degrees is mother-warm
and the coach, a silent giant, calls me Ma'am.
He apologizes because the water is cloudy.
O my chlorinated Mediterranean! Hold me!
I rock across that cradle, a shipwreck
for twenty laps, then haul myself on deck
back in the impossible freight of my body.

Body that housed you, but now claims no right
except in this snapshot on the window ledge
of a borrowed parlor where a diamond bit
the glass to save a man's name from the dark.
It's last summer in this picture, a day on the edge
of our time zone. We are standing in the park,

our genes declare themselves, death smiles in the sun
streaking the treetops, the sky all lightstruck. . . .
In the dark you were packed about with toys,
you were sleeping on your knees, never alone
your breathing making little o's
of trust, night smooth as soapstone
and the hump of your bottom like risen bread. . . .

Darling, Belgian citizen, I put away my dread
but things knock at the elephant legs of this house.
In the bump of pipes there thunders the horse
who kicked you in the face the year you were eleven.
The welt on your cheek raised up round and even
as a biscuit, and we had no ice, but put
a block of frozen meat to it. Still
I see the scar come up in certain lights
when you're at the window, thin as a pencil.

Let the joists of this house endure their dry rot.
Let termites push under them in their blind tunnels
thoughtfully chewing. I chew on the knot
we were once. Meanwhile, your eyes, serene
in the photo, look most thoughtfully out
and could be bullet holes, or beauty spots.

TO SWIM, TO BELIEVE
Centre College, Danville, Kentucky

The beautiful excess of Jesus on the waters
is with me now in the Boles Natatorium.
This bud of me exults, giving witness:

these flippers that rose up to be arms.
These strings drawn to be fingers.
Legs plumped to make my useful fork.

Each time I tear this seam to enter,
all that I carry is taken from me,
shucked in the dive.

Lovers, children, even words go under.
Matters of dogma spin off in the freestyle
earning that mid-pool spurt, like faith.

Where have I come from? Where am I going?
What do I translate, gliding back and forth
erasing my own stitch marks in this lane?

Christ on the lake was not thinking
where the next heel-toe went.
God did him a dangerous favor

whereas Peter, the thinker, sank.

The secret is in the relenting,
the partnership. I let my body work

accepting the dangerous favor
from this king-size pool of waters.
Together I am supplicant. I am bride.

THE SELLING OF THE SLAVES

Lexington, Kentucky

The brood mares on the block at Tipton Pavilion
have ears as delicate as wineglass stems.
Their eyes roll up and out like china dolls'.
Dark red petals flutter in their nostrils.
They are a strenuous ballet, the thrust and suck
of those flanks, and meanwhile the bags of foals
joggle, each pushing against its knapsack.

They are brought on one at a time, worked over
in the confines of a chain-link silver tether
by respectful attendants in white jackets
and blackface. The stage manager hovers
in the background with a gleaming shovel
and the air ripens with the droppings he dips up.

In the velvet pews a white-tie congregation
fans itself with the order of the service.
Among them pass the prep-school deacons
in blazers and the emblems of their districts.
Their hymnals are clipboards. The minister
in an Old Testament voice recites
a liturgy of bloodlines. Ladies and Gentlemen:

Hip Number 20 is Rich and Rare
a consistent and highclass producer.
She is now in foal to that good horse, Brazen.
Candy Dish slipped twins on January one
and it is with genuine regret I must announce
that Roundabout, half sister to a champion,
herself a dam of winners, is barren this season.

She is knocked down at eleven thousand dollars
to the man from Paris with a diamond in his tooth,
the man from Paris with a snake eye in his collar.

When money changes hands among men of worth
it is all done with sliding doors and decorum
but snake whips slither behind the curtain.
In the vestry flasks go round. The gavel's
report is a hollow gunshot:
sold, old lady! and the hot
manure of fear perfumes God's chapel.

NIGHT SOIL

for Wendell Berry, despite inaccuracies

The poet, a hill man, curses
machinery. Cars run over his dogs.
Tractors balk, slip into reverse
or threaten to tip over on the slopes.
Except for a pickup truck to take
him down to the river bottom place,
he works by animal, gee-upping
behind an old Thoroughbred mare
he got last year in a swap.
She's sweet enough, except some days
her ancestry speaks up
and she takes him breakneck downhill.
This is the kind of shop
we talk, he telling me how
the plod went out of plowing back
when farmers changed over
from cud-chewers. Right now,
admiring the clover-
shaped harness burn
he's wearing down one cheek
I tell him that a pair of oxen
could put the trudge back in.

A man with eyes bluer
than his Kentucky sky ponds
that leach out of the limestone undertow
wherever the land puckers to form a saucer,
his god is in the furrow.
He wants to put back in the earth
something of what he takes from it.
Hence his privy, built into a hill,
conforms to a theory as roundabout
as the Japanese tending their night soil.

Before the sun goes down, I enter it,
a room still bleeding pine rosin,
the latrine of an intellectual.
Almost due south of where I sit
the cows, impatient to be stanchioned,
are lowing. At the trough, pigs mew away.
There's a stack of quarterlies
at eye level. They say:
we read where we can,
but my own words spring up
from the top magazine!
I am undone.
The cows are to be milked,
pigs to be swilled.
I find myself in the outhouse
and am emptied
and am filled.

PAIRING THE GEESE ON
MY FORTY-NINTH BIRTHDAY

The gosling's eye is lidless
and navy blue.
A series of shutters clicks in it.
Yellow flecks, like plankton,
swim over the flutter.
I, who am in fact new
to this business, look in
on the morning of June six
and see my own pale embryo
chipping away with its egg tooth.

The gosling's sex is deeply kept.
Under its feathers
a sort of button lurks.
I squeeze around it as if
to open a pimple
and expose a shy, two-way conduit,
a male-female look-alike
tunnel of nursery pink
except the penis, if one is intended,
will pop up in it.

My other hand, meanwhile,
strokes the gosling's breast

to keep it sootheful on its back
while being sexed.
These are my birthday birds,
gift from a neighbor's hatch.

We kneel to our work, agreeing
it's demeaning but not cruel.
Six birds later, each squirting upward,
feces dribbling on my shirt, her shirt,
the unmistakable gander stands forth.

How mildly each one permits
this upending!
Head on a swivel, it watches.
Its docked wings lie down
like elbow stumps so that
my goslings, once I've paired them,
will not flap up from the pond
where they've been planted
to decorate the surface,
to honk with their white trumpets,
to come, in the slippage of my days,
of mating age,
preening each other's feathers,
eating each other's lice.

IN THE ROOT CELLAR

The parsnips, those rabbis
have braided their beards together
to examine the text. The word
that engrosses them is: February.

To be a green tomato
wrapped in the Sunday book section
is to know nothing. Meanwhile
the wet worm eats his way outward.

These cabbages, these clean keepers
in truth are
a row of impacted stillbirths.
One by one we deliver them.

The apples are easy abutters
a basket of pulltoys and smiles.
Still, they infect one another
like children exchanging the measles.

O potato, a wink of
daylight and you're up with
ten tentative erections.
How they deplete you!

Dusty blue wart hogs, the squash
squat for a thump and a tuning.
If we could iron them out
they'd be patient blue mandolins.

The beets wait wearing their birthmarks.
They will be wheeled into the amphitheater.
Even before the scrub-up, the scalpel,
they bleed a little.

I am perfect, breathes the onion.
I am God's first circle
the tulip that slept in His navel.
Bite me and be born.

IN THE PINE GROVE

I sleepwalk at high noon
in an abandoned arcade.
The silence is heavier than telephone poles
and the light has been washed thin
with Seconal. If music
played here, its high note
was fear carried off by a chickadee.
The floor is a sidewalk of fallen hair.
Once it was wheat-colored
but age has rusted it.
In this place of underpinnings
the only green is the toupee of treetops.
The only birds are migrants off course.
No stones. No hideaways of grubs.
Only little faces push through the dark,
little mushroom ghosts who have put
both feet into one trouser leg.

THE DIARY KEEPER

to remember T. H. White

I speak to the loneliness of the diary keeper
holing up for months at a time
in some cottage abutting a haybarn
always at an altitude where
the valley folk appear like black fleas
in the snow and the grouse go up
in a flurry of extra heartbeats.

In phrases lazy as marriage
running on, breaking off, beginning again
he tells me the geese are flying,
the dogs have run down a deer,
the pipes in the kitchen are frozen
but the fire comes forth in the morning,
leather softens, spring is a dazzling absence
and later, the bitch has whelped too soon.
I drowned seven; I won't
exorcise this shame with words
but feel it.

I would speak to the man turned inward
mending and making do,
his entries like visits clumsily spaced
as he pries words up out of Latin,
patches a flannel shirt and wishes

---

for *a sewing machine, an auto-giro,*
the Oxford English Dictionary,
all the while throwing up bridges
across his God-fired rages,
griefs smothered under the coal scuttle,
quilts laid over the long winter drunks,
the carouses, the sick melancholic forenoons

and never a word of woman, never
a word of those ovals, those olives,
those teacups unpoured and untasted.

The reader I am is a woman
(though solitude makes no distinction, sir,
in the rootstock) and given
like you to the winter habit of thinking.
On a day when the snow falls all cross-eyed
and the woodstove spits out its caulkings
and scattering hay to the ponies, the pitchfork
raises a mouse on one prong
I follow you into your housepride
in the heart of your red-and-white kitchen,

the ferment of your bachelor salvages,
to say that I too *would be more of*
a coward if I had the courage

and coward, come muffled,
come gaitered like you
come waving a fifth of Kilkenny Irish
to mourn you into your due date.

INSOMNIA

—To hear the owl is the poet's prerogative.

In the hand-me-down of dead hours
I hear him moving up the mountain
tree by tree insistent as
a paranoid calling out his one verse
raising the break-bone alarm like
those quaint East European churches
that tolled their non-Sunday bells
to usher in the pogrom.

Finally he settles in my basswood.
We both doze listening for each other.
Going out to help my horse up
in the first light I see him
hurry into the haymow
furtive as an old boarder
flapping along the corridor
to tell his secret to the toilet.

O red eye! Sit tight
up in the rafters.
Hang on
safe as a puffball.
Tonight
another chapter—
the promise of hatchets.

THE MUMMIES

Two nights running I was out there
in orange moonlight with old bedsheets
and a stack of summered-over Sunday papers
tucking up the tomatoes while the peppers
whimpered and went under and the radishes
dug in with their dewclaws and all over
the field the goldenrod blackened
and fell down like Napoleon's army.

This morning they're still at it, my tomatoes
making marbles, making more of those little
green volunteers that you can rattle
all winter in a coat pocket, like fingers.
But today on the lip of the solstice
I will pull them, one hundred
big blind greenies. I will stand them
in white rows in the root cellar
wrapped one by one
in the terrible headlines.

IN THE COMPANY OF TREES

This is the willow.
Consider the tops of her elephant toes
the gazelle sweep of her branches
the mouse eyes of her catkins
and how she translates the sunlight
into an oasis all camels would favor.
Stay close at nightfall
and watch how she is devoured
when the killer porcupine comes
to munch on his giant apple.

Beech is a bakeshop
open all winter. Its leaves
are cinnamon cornucopias
that fill up with snow.
Its nanny girth is smooth
as sausage skin
is durable as butcher cloth.
At times I press my face
to it.

He'll fondle you, this one
old bull pine uncle
with his nicotine fingers.
The kiss of his needles

a shoebrush mustache.
The stains on his waistcoat
a sticky rosin.
He is ringed with young green hearts
his bastard sons.

Thin as Bombay beggars
the birch and the popple
come in in a season
to squat on the unmowed field.
Such a flutter of fingers!
Such light bones
the hatchet sings them down
in one note.

The elms die but are buried upright
like Parsees.
Sloughs of bark
lie at their feet, a batch
of undelivered letters.
Their side seams gape.
Everyone lives in these crannies.
The flickers have picked out
a textbook in Braille.
The raccoons have scribbled graffiti.
It is a dusty holding
except in the January thaw when
a host of Old Velvet Foot comes forth
a congregation of sweet wet mushrooms
nodding their caps
in prayer.

ON DIGGING OUT OLD LILACS

I stand in a clump of dead athletes.
They have been buried upright
in Olympic poses. One
a discobolus clutching a bird's nest.
One a runner trailing laces of snakeskin.
One a boxer exploding toads of cracked leather.

I call in the hatchet, the mattock, the crowbar
the dog with his tines for
the trick is to get at the taproot.
Each one is as thick as a weightlifter's thigh.

First you must rupture those handholds but
each has a stone in its fist.
Each one encloses beetles that pinch
like aroused crabs. Some
will not relax even when
bludgeoned about the neckbone.

Next you must chip up kneecaps and scapulas.
Knuckles and hammertoes fly in the dustbin
until on my hands and knees
I ring something metal. An ox shoe

hatched underground for a hundred years
a gristle of earth in its mouth.

I see them at the pasture wall
the great dumb pair
imperfectly yoked and straining
straining at the stone boat and
meanwhile the shoe in my hand
its three prongs up on the half-moon.

It is enough that the lilacs must go,
a mess of broken bones in the gully.
I give the shoe back to the earth
for now I am a woman
in a long-gone dooryard
flinging saved dishwater onto
these new slips.

A TIME FOR THE EATING OF GRASSES

Let the likes of this begin
in the glut of May
when the heavy white geese come
single file on comic feet
back to the pond from their winter pen.
Tweezing the long-haired grass
they tick left right
like a conga line of metronomes
that have skidded out of sync.

Let it move on to the lambs
who smile the eternal smiles
of mongoloid children, the smiles
of the always tethered who nip
close to the cuticle
pulling tufts from the dusty scurf.
At the least shock they huddle
eyes shut heads down rumps up
tight as a football team.

Allow it to cover the calm
sidewise chewing of cows
who wear their flies like black tears

with the patience of foragers
and horses who scour the browse
with porous noses living at the pinch
until the shut-in time of stanchions and pens
when what will come comes
at the whim of man.

Let it end with the goat
carrying his ears
like empty cornucopias
the goat still stripping brush
after the blight of frost
or when the blanket comes down
debarking logs in the woodpile.
Goat a factory of himself
a fermentation vat
spilling the beebee shot wastes
out of the basket of his rectum
goat the survival artist.

IV

SONG FOR SEVEN PARTS OF THE BODY

1.

This one,
a common type,
turns in.
Was once attached.
Fed me as sweetly
as an opium pipe.
O, birthdays unlimber us,
eyes sit back,
ears go indoors,
but here nothing changes.
This was.
This is.

2.

Mostly they lie low
put up shells, sprout hairs
and if they sing, they know
only leather cares.
Blind marchers five abreast
left, right
silent as mushrooms or puff paste
they rise up free at night.

3.

I have a life of my own
he says. He is transformed
without benefit of bone.
I will burrow, he says
and enters. Afterwards
he goes slack as a slug.
He remembers little.
The prince is again a frog.

4.

Here is a field that never lies fallow.
Sweat waters it, nails hoe the roots.
Every day death comes in with the winnow.
Every day newborns crop up like asparagus.
At night, all night on the pillow
you can hear the narrow sprouts crackle
rubbing against each other,
lying closer than lemmings.
They speak to their outposts in armpits.
They speak to their settlers in crotches.
Neighbor, neighbor, they murmur.

5.

They have eyes that see not.
They straddle the valley of wishes.
Their hills make their own rules.
Among them are bobbers

melons, fishes
doorknobs and spools.
At times they whisper, touch me.

6.

Imagine a mouth
without you, pink man,
goodfellow.
A house
without a kitchen,
a fishless ocean.
No way to swallow.

7.

These nubbins
these hangers-on
hear naught.
Wise men
tug them in thought.
Lovers
may nibble each other's.
Maidens
gypsies and peasants
make holes in theirs
to hang presents.

THE LEG

I thought I had you memorized, good fellow.
At the ankle knob two bright veins
used to thrum as fine as blue guitar strings.
There was the flat blade of the shin canting
over the hard pillow
of a swimmer's calf. Above it, plain
as the nose on my face, a bony knee.
And up into the root there ran
a fleshy thigh, that serviceable tree,
one half the common plan.

Now after three months they turn you loose.
The doctor, stepping into a plastic sou'wester,
begins to saw through plaster
and the white dust flies from my great oxhorn.
Wrapped toe to fork, a poor wrong fetus,
you were the big baby I carried everywhere
impatient to be born,
impossible to bear,
a dingy shut-in with one window on the square.

They coast me off to X-ray, an embarrassment.
So I'm to take you back, a wasted eel,

hairy and hapless, yet somehow attached.
You waggle in the wheelchair, scaly and spent.
You can't attend a single simple rule.
Bending's a desperate forgotten habit.
To move at all you must be flexed
by hand. Stretched out you tremble
at the least touch like a snared rabbit.

Come, little one. They say you're tough as leather.
They say you've knit, the worst is over.
I'll crutch you home and we'll lie down together.
The way long absence works refining lovers
will work in you, my shrunken stalk.
Come summer and we'll walk.

THE ETERNAL LOVER

The last grasshoppers
thinner than political prisoners
breast up out of the goldenrod.
They know they are flying into
the end of the journey.
Toads in their outsize skins
doze on stones. They line up
like old men in lumpy sweaters
sunning themselves outside
the art museum
taking what they can get.
Meanwhile the woodchuck
is dragging his rusty heartbeat
deep under the granite ledges.
He will be dreamless all winter.

The lover, shaving,
consults his mirror.
Last night's dream stands behind him
all teeth and mouth and legs.
He is a natty dresser, but
it is that season for him, too.
For twenty years he has lain
with legions of golden girls
alike as polka dots

each with a gift-wrapped face
each with a butterfly mouth
to be planted under his tongue.
As long as one virgin alights on
the edge of the East Side penthouse
the world is his cocktail party.
He sips from the plastic champagne glass.
He has much to consider.

Meanwhile Mother on Elm Street
verboten in her corset
can be seen lying on the rooftop
can be seen hammering down the shingles
can be seen spilling out the honey
can be seen savaging the carpet.
In one frame she cries clumsily
her tears loose as gumdrops
her mouth pulled down like a rubber band.
Meanwhile he is required
to make ineffectual love to
his first girl over and over
the Jessie, the joy of his hometown.
He undresses her under the bleachers.
Armed to the teeth with entreaties
he replays that fearsome scrimmage
of buttons and bra straps and stockings
dreaming the same dream the same dream

while grasshoppers rise in the tall weeds
to take their last lap in the pasture
like cross-country hurdlers.

RUNNING AWAY TOGETHER

It will be an island on strings
well out to sea and austere
bobbing as if at anchor
green with enormous fir trees
formal as telephone poles.

We will arrive there slowly
hand over hand without oars.
Last out, you will snip the fragile
umbilicus white as a beansprout
that sewed us into our diaries.

We will be two bleached hermits
at home in our patches and tears.
We will butter the sun with our wisdom.
Our days will be grapes on a trellis
perfectly oval and furred.

At night we will set our poems
adrift in ginger ale bottles
each with a clamshell rudder
each with a piggyback spider
waving them off by dogstar

and nothing will come from the mainland
to tell us who cares, who cares
and nothing will come of our lovelock
except as our two hearts go soft
and black as avocado pears.

HEAVEN AS ANUS

In the Defense Department there is a shop
where scientists sew the eyelids of rabbits open
lest they blink in the scorch of a nuclear drop

and elsewhere dolphins are being taught to defuse
bombs in the mock-up of a harbor and monkeys
learn to perform the simple tasks of draftees.

It is done with electric shocks. Some mice
who have failed their time tests in the maze
now go to the wire unbidden for their jolts.

Implanting electrodes yields rich results:
alley cats turn from predators into prey.
Show them a sparrow and they cower

while the whitewall labs fill up with the feces of fear
where calves whose hearts have been done away
with walk and bleat on plastic pumps.

And what is any of this to the godhead,
these squeals, whines, writhings, unexpected jumps,
whose children burn alive, booby-trap the dead,
lop ears and testicles, core and disembowel?

It all ends at the hole. No words may enter
the house of excrement. We will meet there
as the sphincter of the good Lord opens wide
and He takes us all inside.

YOUNG NUN AT BREAD LOAF

Sister Elizabeth Michael
has come to the Writers' Conference.
She has white habits like a summer sailor
and a black notebook she climbs into nightly
to sway in the hammock of a hundred knotted poems.
She is the youngest nun I have ever known.

When we go for a walk in the woods
she puts on a dimity apron that teases her boottops.
It is sprigged with blue flowers.
I wear my jeans and sneakers. We are looking
for mushrooms (chanterelles are in season)
to fry and eat with my drinks, her tomato juice.

Wet to the shins with crossing
and recrossing the same glacial brook, a mile
downstream we find them, the little pistols,
denser than bandits among the tree roots.
Forager, she carries the basket.
Her hands are crowded with those tough yellow thumbs.

Hiking back in an unction of our own sweat
she brings up Christ. Christ, that canard!

I grind out a butt and think of the waiting bourbon.
The sun goes down in disappointment.
You can say what you want, she says.
You live as if you believe.

Sister
Sister Elizabeth Michael
says we are doing Christ's work, we two.
She, the rosy girl in a Renoir painting.
I, an old Jew.

THE HORSEWOMAN

It is said to begin with the father
who is strong with a mustache
and a full mouth as bright as a semaphore
mixing up kisses with rages.
Nothing contains his breathing.
The triphammer of his chest
strains even the best suitcloth.
Hairs grow from his knuckles.
The crop is stuck in his right boot.

And here comes the loving cup lady
leading her Thoroughbred.
They are a perfect fit.
She loves his sweat.
Sweetly she wheels his manure
down the barn floor
and sweetly into the ring
he lifts the proud startle
of his great feet
highest of all the fliers
over the spines of fences.

All this for her daddy—
the scrape of the curry

the sweat strap, the hoofpick
the pyramid droppings.
All this for her daddy—
the banging on iron
the foaming on leather.

She returns at a trot for her ribbon
with her slim neck and good teeth
with her hair wayward in the wind.
Reins slack, leaning back in the saddle
she comes on like a messenger
to the king.

All this for the fantasy daddy
that princely blackboot
when in fact the bona fide father
hunkered over his bourbon
and never went out of doors
except to dry out on the cure
or begin again with AA
on Coke and straight water
and kept his indifferent eyes away
from his wishbone of a daughter.

THE HERO

It was those Snake Creek veins
standing out on his temples, blue
as Waterman's Ink, the true
murk color of anger
swelling with all they contained
saying Caution, Danger;

it was those veins on the face
of your giant, your father the druggist
that thirty years downstream still twist
their vine ropes in your head.
And you the hero of this place
carpenter, boss of the plumb bob lead

whose eyes like his will be knotholes
whose bones like his small sticks
man of his blood, master of his tricks
consider. Consider these acts of grace:
Let us wrap words up in dumplings
and eat of them, exchanging bowls.

Let us butter our fingers, those ten dumb things
to spread on the crackers of old men
bring genius a cognac, a school
of quick goldfish for the fool
before we are nothing again.

THE BAD TRIP

The leopard frogs are chuckling in the dark.
The sky holds up a brand-new zodiac
and a diesel crossing the creek sends back
its wolf cry. We are sitting in a warm room
open to the turpentine of trees.
The wine goes round, and with it go these
stick fingers of stick men—Cambodian
contraband wrapped up in paper flags,
your flag and mine. The game is: Turning On.

Dreaming awake, I see the shapes of things
thicken their outlines like a Rouault painting.
The centers grow so clear they self-destruct.
The hi-fi thumps on a vault of underthoughts.
The offbeat bursts its doors, all locks unlock
and spaces hand-to-hand attenuate.
They sting like burned skin. Distances pivot.
The time that measures words yaws like a Yo-yo.
Someone speaks in my mouth. I admire the trick.
We are good children! We love one another! We all go
riding the wind's back to a dear republic.

But later, alone, I've played the game too well.
My heart hammers a hole from inside out.
Sparklers from a child's July needle
my eyes, start fires, will not be blinked shut.
Four things that were my arms and legs die down.
Porous enough to float, they are old stones.
The fingers are falling from this icy leper
but the mind hangs on spinning like a hot star.

I am afraid in three languages. I am
shipwrecked in poor French, beached in bad Russian,
cast up like a grain sack. *J'ai peur.* Old terrors come,
not one too small or secret to take in.
I am back at the local firehouse. I watch
the dogs dragged in on skidding toenails, one
by one, for their rabies shots. The floor's awash
with Pinesol, vomit, and the urine of fear.
They know as much as I, and I know nothing.
It doesn't end. The cornered dogs are here.

And then you hold me. You, outside my tunnel,
my dark drownings, the knife thrower at the fair,
the noose, the ice fall, the starved hounds in the kennel.
You, crawling my long crawl out of the nightmare.

IN THE UNEASY SLEEP
OF THE TRANSLATOR

With a broad shoehorn
I am unstuffing a big bird in this dream
—somebody else's holiday feast—
and repacking the crop of my own,
knowing it will burst with such
onion, oyster, savory bread crust.

I see in the dream they are someone's poems
to be wrested from an elliptic French.
A woman like me, her lines heavy with lovers,
locked churches, Saturday traffic jams.
When we meet on a park bench
in the Tuileries' frame I discover
her face is narrow and shy,
a nuthatch's, perhaps, tinted blue.
She runs headfirst down an ash tree.

Meanwhile her high heels click.
Her eyes are elusive, all-seeing,
her thighs fishlike,
her dress stressed at the seams.
My words wear the vapid smiles of cows
grazing along the text
on Alps of edelweiss.

I collapse her poems like rows
of chairs arranged for cheap funerals,
saying, see here, my friend,
my double, let us breathe
mouth to mouth like a lifesaving class
as chockful and as brave
forcefeeding each other's stopped lungs
so that at the feast of words
there will be no corpse to carve.

SAYING GOOD-BY

We kissed in the car in
the Howard Johnson parking lot
while the french fries, pale
as erasers in the take-out box,
oiled each other's wet sides
and the bland magnesia milkshake
belched secretly under its straws.
The slats of the aqua cupola
were sharply watchful.
A thin sleet salted the orange roof.

At that time a swollen woman,
her hair in pink snakes heavier
than Medusa's, cornered herself
in the phone booth and worked
at the holes of the dial.
She spoke. Her alarm was a dumb show
of large gestures and she heaved
herself out as from an execution
and started down the state highway,
the young girl inside her running.

The telephone dangled on its cord,
hapless as a shoe swayed by its laces,
and the howler signal sang
until it entered our own mouths.

THE FAINT-HEARTED SUICIDE

Where the arm
narrows down to its human part
where the skin
lilts over its rivers
smooth as old beach glass
and ten underground thongs
tie the palm in place
tie the base
of the leg-o'-mutton thumb
that squat wise man
in position

there at that gentle confluence
two worms
not exactly twins
sleep in their white welts
sleep ragged but uncurled
under the scars
where X marks the spot.

I finger it left to right.
I have it by heart
that white night:

the bathroom bulb a hot eye
the square white tiles
heaving against you
the shower rail dripping teeth
life at your temples
setting the time bomb
while the helpless towels
huddle in a corner
and the brand-new Wilkinson blade
winks out of the razor.

I think of the sweet streets
of your childhood—
Upsal, Tulpehocken, Queen's Lane—
an alphabet of old place names
tucked into your bicycle.
I think of those summer nights
spread wide as a platter
with the trumpet vines drowsing
their way up the veranda
and the porch swing a scratchy flute
answering the cicadas.

There was a bed made for you
there was a durable kitchen
where almonds and apricots
knocked in the cupboards
there were waxed newel posts
footsteps that listened and loved you

UP FROM THE EARTH

I am sucking my teeth to keep
shut against the blackflies.
They stagger out of the furrow
like coffee grounds magicked alive
to walk on my eyeballs
and flap past my nose hairs
and homestead in the snailholes of my ears.
If I speak they enter in droves.
Going down they are lightly salted.

Meanwhile the wet burls of earthworms
pink as the fat lady's garter
arise as plain as a whisper
sent up from the prompter's box.
All of the toads are wearing
Goodwill overcoats. They turn
out their torn pockets.

Inside each Merrimack packet
the seeds wait for their lineup:
coral chaff that will be carrots,
black nits that will bloom as lettuce,
pale cobbles of beets, the surprise

of pink beads that will put up
the moon faces of cauliflower.
Only the green bean does not pretend
and corn can look like itself.

Turning the garden I thank
Bishop Ockham for his pin
crowded with dancing angels
as in my noiseless saliva
a million microbes breed.
And thank you, patient Amanda,
for the engine of your digestion
yielding these pure rank
bushels of horse manure
that slept here all winter
a blanket on a blanket.

AMANDA IS SHOD

The way the cooked shoes sizzle
dropped in a pail of cold water
the way the coals in the portable forge
die out like hungry eyes
the way the nails go in aslant
each one the tip of a snake's tongue

and the look of the parings
after the farrier's knife
has sliced through.

I collect them
four marbled white C's
as refined as petrified wood
and dry them to circles of bone
and hang them away on my closet hook

lest anyone cast a spell on Amanda.

AMANDA DREAMS SHE HAS DIED AND GONE TO THE ELYSIAN FIELDS

This morning Amanda
lies down during breakfast.
The hay is hip high.
The sun sleeps on her back
as it did on the spine
of the dinosaur
the fossil bat
the first fish with feet
she was once.
A breeze fans
the deerflies from lighting.
Only a gaggle of gnats
housekeeps in her ears.
A hay plume sticks out of her mouth.

I come calling with a carrot
from which I have taken
the first bite.
She startles
she considers rising
but retracts the pistons
of her legs and accepts
as loose-lipped as a camel.

We sit together.
In this time and place
we are heart and bone.
For an hour
we are incorruptible.

THE AGNOSTIC SPEAKS
TO HER HORSE'S HOOF

Come, frog, reveal yourself.
Surface out of the poultice
the muck and manure pack.
Make your miraculous V to stand up.
Show me as well the tickle place
that cleft between.

The Good Book says a man's life
is as grass the wind passes over
and is gone.
According to the *National Geographic*
the oceans will lie down dead
as cesspools in sixty years.

Let us ripen in our own way—
I with my back to the trunk
of a butternut that has caught
the fatal red canker
and on my knee
this skillet of your old foot.

The hoofpick is God's instrument
as much as I know of Him.

In my hands let it raise
your moon, Amanda, your nerve bone.
Let us come to the apocalypse complete
without splinter or stone.
Let us ride out
on four iron feet.

EYES

At night Amanda's eyes
are rage red with toy worlds inside.
Head on they rummage the dark
of the paddock like twin cigars
but flicker at the edges with
the shyer tongues of the spirit lamp.

There's little enough for her to see:
my white shirt, the sleeves
rolled high, two flaps of stale bread
in my fish paws. I can't sleep.
I have come back from
the feed-bag-checkered restaurant
from the pale loose tears of my dearest friend
her blue eyes sinking into the highball glass
her eyeballs clinking on ice
and her mouth drawn down in the grand
comedy of anguish.

Today a sparrow has been put
in the hawk's hands and in the net
a monarch crazes its wings on gauze.
A doe run down by the dogs

commonly dies of fright before
its jugular opens at the fang hole.
In my friend's eyes the famine victim
squats, holding an empty rice bowl.

O Amanda, burn out my dark.
Press the warm suede of your horseflesh
against my cold palm.
Take away all that is human.

THE SUMMER OF THE WATERGATE HEARINGS

I wake in New Hampshire.
The sun is still withheld.
For six days Amanda has stood
through drizzles and downpours.

This morning she steams.
Little pyramids of her droppings
surround her. Dead worms
shine in them like forgotten

spaghetti, proof she has eaten
the sugar-coated cure.
Four dozen ascarids, ten strongyles—
I count them to make sure.

And all the while in Washington
worms fall out of the government
pale as the parasites that drain
from the scoured gut of my mare.

They blink open on the television screen.
Night after night on the re-run
I count them to make sure.

BRUSHING THE AUNTS

Consider Amanda, my sensible strawberry roan,
her face with its broad white blaze
lending an air of constant surprise.
Homely Amanda, colossal and mild.
She evokes those good ghosts of my childhood
brillo-haired and big-boned,
the freckled maiden aunts.
Though barren like her, they were not petulant.

Peaceable dears, they lay down alone
mute as giraffes in my mother's house,
fed tramps on the back porch
after The Crash,
pantomimed the Charleston
summer nights in the upstairs back bedroom
and dropped apple peels over their shoulders
to spell the name of a marrying man.

Remembering this,
I bring Amanda windfalls.
That season again.
The power of the leaf runs the human brain
raising the dead like lamb clouds in the sky.

The power of the thorn holds the birds' late nests
now strung like laundry from the blackberry canes
where parts of Amanda recur.
Her body fuzz is stickered in the oriole cups.
Copper hairs from her tail hang the packages up.

All fall as I drop to the scalp of sleep
while the raccoons whistle
and the geese cough
and Amanda grows small in my head,
the powder streak of her face a blur
seventy pastures off,
the aunts return letting down their hair.
It hangs to the custard of Harriet's lap.
It tickles the spine of Alma's girdle
and the dream unwinds like a top.

In 4/4 time the way it was once
I am brushing the carrot frizz gone gray
a hundred ritual strokes one way,
a hundred ritual strokes the other.
We dance the old back-bedroom dance
that rattles the shakes of my mother's house
till Amanda jitters yanking her tether,
her eyes green holes in the dark, her blaze
a slice of moon looming at the gate
and the latch flies up on another night.

THINKING OF DEATH AND DOGFOOD

Amanda, you'll be going
to Alpo or to Gaines
when you run out of luck;
the flesh flensed from your bones
your mammoth rib cage rowing
away to the renderer's
a dry canoe on a truck

while I foresee my corpse
slid feet first into fire
light as the baker's loaf
to make of me at least
a pint of potash spoor.
I'm something to sweeten the crops
when the clock hand stops.

Amanda, us in the woods
miles from home, the ground
upending in yellow flutes
that open but make no sound.
Ferns in the mouth of the brute,
chanterelles in the woman's sack . . .
what do I want for myself

dead center, bareback
on the intricate harp of your spine?
All that I name as mine

with the sure slow oxen of words:
feed sacks as grainy as boards
that air in the sun. A boy
who is wearing my mother's eyes.
Garlic to crush in the pan.
The family gathering in.
Already in the marsh
the yearling maples bleed
a rich onrush. Time slips
another abacus bead.

Let it not stick in the throat
or rattle a pane in the mind.
May I leave no notes behind
wishful, banal or occult
and you, small thinker in
the immensity of your frame
may you be caught and crammed
midmouthful of the best grain
when the slaughterer's bullet slams
sidelong into your brain.

Please Do Not Remove Card From Pocket

YOUR LIBRARY CARD
may be used at all library agencies. You
are, of course, responsible for all materials
checked out on it. As a courtesy to others
please return materials promptly — before
overdue penalties are imposed.

The SAINT PAUL PUBLIC LIBRARY

DEMCO